Elsabeth's Dance

A SHOALMAN CHRONICLES STORY

KIRA DECKER

Elsabeth's Dance: A Shoalman Chronicles Story

The Shoalman Chronicles Series

Copyright 2020 © by Kira Decker

ISBN: 978-1-7376864-0-8

Happy Reading!

Dedication

To my loving husband, who danced into my life right when I needed him.

Table of Contents

Part I

The Present

Death faced Rockshoalman.

Others might recoil and flee in fear, but after five hundred years, death's ability to intimidate him had lost its power.

Except here.

Darkness surrounded him, cold and unfeeling, the moon cowering behind the patchy clouds as if afraid to intrude. Only his breath leaving trails of silver vapor in the air proved life existed amongst the ruins. Nestled on the highest peak of the parish lands, the manse sat high on a cliff overlooking the local village in the valley below. Rockshoalman stepped gingerly toward the edge, careful in the lamplight not to lose his footing on the dew swept stone— although not even that fall could kill him.

Traditional wood and stone houses stretched out before him. Gas lamps lined the village streets, twinkles of light against a midnight black canvas. A hundred years ago it had been the same. The village and surrounding area—much like himself—remained ageless against time. Wisps of music floated on the air. The inhabitants celebrating in the local pub most likely; the day forgotten in drink and song. Forgotten like him.

The click of the caretaker's gnarled wooden cane against the cobblestone paths turned Rockshoalman towards the two-story manse once more. No such life reached the stone manor house remnants before him. The multi-hued and speckled granite now dull and muddy in the tentative moonlight. Weathered and rotting boards covered the first-floor windows like haunted eyes peering across the expansive and overgrown front lawn, while withered ivy strangled the two Roman columns in a death grip. It could be the subject of one of his paintings—the kind his curse forced him to paint. The ones he despised.

Despair reached its insidious fingers around his heart, abrading the hope he clung to in desperation. Rockshoalman stared at the horse-drawn carriage, the only means of transportation to the manse he could procure, and the uncertain future it offered. Could he be free to live if the shadows of his past remained?

"This is a mistake," he whispered to the icy wind tugging at his navy blue, wool overcoat. "I should not have returned."

With a heavy sigh, he resigned himself to a half-life. Before he took more than a step towards the carriage, the moon escaped past the clouds to cast a pale moonbeam on a splash of color. His breath caught.

A single pink bloom graced the otherwise barren flower garden that edged the cobblestone path leading towards the front entrance. Life challenged death.

She is here.

Kneeling, Rockshoalman picked the peony. Cradled within his palm, the floral scent swelled around him, edging the darkness away with happier thoughts. The layers of petals reminded him of the lace and ruffles of a time a hundred years past. He sighed and tucked the flower into his lapel. The kernel of hope within his heart dared to flare brighter.

"Not sure this is a good idea," the gruff voice of the estate's caretaker complained as the old man reached his side.

"Nothing can harm me here." Not physically at least. Rockshoalman pushed the morose thought away. Returning here was a risk. If his demon found him, there would be nowhere to run. Provided provoking the past didn't send him into an

abomination   painting   frenzy   first.
Rockshoalman closed his eyes, fighting to
control the memories and the painful guilt of
loss that threatened to allow his curse to
overtake him.

"Why is your Guardian not with ya?"

Rockshoalman glared. The caretaker
blanched almost as pale as his silver hair.

"He has no place here tonight." Only
Ciprian Solvak had set foot on this estate,
and he had died for that choice.

No more Guardian's deaths would
plague his conscience because of the manse.
He had not wanted Lucien Solvak, Ciprian's
great-great-grandson and current Guardian,
haunted by the memories of death

Rockshoalman might experience tonight. No Guardian should have to relive their predecessor's demise.

Only after hours of arguing had Lucien agreed to remain behind. That and a confession. This place was a scar he needed to heal by himself.

For her.

Rockshoalman stood and pointed to the entranceway. "Open the manse."

Hobbling up the front steps, the old man unlocked the padlocked double doors but drew back the hand poised to open them. "Can this not wait 'til morning?"

"No," Rockshoalman stated in a flat tone, his shoulders taut. Ghosts are best faced in the darkness where they dwell.

"Suit yourself." A weatherworn hand turned the brass doorknob on the iron-bound doors and pushed. Hinges shrieked their displeasure at being disturbed. The old man flinched and made a quick sign of the cross.

Rockshoalman ignored him. Long strides carried him to the mahogany spiral staircase, pain infusing each creaky step and crack in the plaster walls until he reached the second-floor landing of the once grand house. Blood pounded in his ears as his heart rammed against his ribs. Rockshoalman fought to control the trembling coursing through his form. The hair on the back of his neck prickled. Power lingered within these walls still—a chill air painted with memories. Echoes of long-gone children's laughter as they ran down the main hallway to his left settled amongst the broken furniture and leaf-strewn debris, the musty scent of mold heavy in the air. The buzz of forgotten voices hovered in the smoke-stained, high dome ceiling over the central curved stairway. Each sound, each smell tearing at his control.

The weight of centuries pressed in. Could he do this? Could he face a past he would rather forget? Except, part of that past, he feared to let go—a death grip that kept him from living. With a ragged breath, he forced himself to push through the gaping maw of the dilapidated grand ballroom.

Running his hands down the carved wood archway, moisture and cold coated his skin along with ageless soot. How long had it been since he last stood here? Almost a century younger at least, yet Rockshoalman's dark Roman-Romani lineage and youthful appearance remained unchanged.

Are you here?

No answers came from the shadows, only the pulse of loss. Mist rose and swirled across the floor. A low moan rumbled, vibrating the ancient oak floors beneath his

11

feet. The very stones of the house groaned in pain. Faces flashed. Young. Old. Remembered laughter turned to screams. Rockshoalman staggered. Heat licked the palm pressed against the old wood for support. Sucking in a breath, he gagged on the putrid scent of burnt flesh and hair. Still, he persisted. One step. Another. With each forgotten memory clawing for release from the dark recesses where he kept them chained, a suffocating need to paint death increased. If he gave in to his curse, the painting would destroy his soul and his future forever.

"Help me," he whispered to the spirits. "I must proceed. To live. For myself and for her. Else we are both lost."

Heart threatening to beat out of his chest, Rockshoalman slipped a smooth quartz agate from his pocket. The stone warmed as he rubbed his thumb back and forth, the healing energy infused into the worry stone by Lucien, giving him the strength to battle emotions he had only recently learned to embrace. Head bowed, the perfume of the pink peony soothed his ravaged mind. A cool breeze caressed his face, drying the beads of sweat on his brow before chasing the fog of guilt out through a crack in the wall. By the time the slow shuffle of the aged caretaker caught up to him, a temporary calm had returned.

"After a hundred years of decay, the local kommuner wants to demolish the entire place as an eyesore within the month." Flickering lantern light cast harsh shadows upon the flame-kissed beams of the caved-in roof and rubble strewn across the expansive room.

"A century ago, the manse was the jewel of this small, quiet village," Rockshoalman lamented.

"Aye, but no longer."

Behind the layers of soot and dust, brass chandeliers now lay festooned with cobwebs instead of candles. The crystals adorning the many branches dirty and lifeless, yet glimmers of moonlight sneaking through cracks in the boarded-up windows set an odd bright spark dancing across the walls and floor. As though the crystals clung to the hope they might once again dance free.

"You must decide soon. Or the Councillors will choose for you."

Rockshoalman nodded. "Go wait by the carriage. I need to be alone."

"As you wish, Domnule."

Domnule. A Romani title of respect and perhaps, a final plea for Rockshoalman to leave. The footsteps hesitated for a moment longer before the click of the caretaker's cane disappeared into the distance.

Rockshoalman shivered as ghosts from the past kissed his skin in the moonlit silence. This time, the spirits beckoned him. Had they understood his plea? Closing his eyes, Rockshoalman let the walls of the ruined manor house fade. Lilting strains of a forgotten melody grew stronger. Only he heard it, but that was enough to transport him to another place, another time.

Back to her.

Part II

The Past

"Why did you insist I dress tonight?" Rockshoalman tugged at the high, stiff collar of his starched shirt. Ciprian batted his hand away.

Standing in the grand entranceway of the Danish castle, muted conversations and glancing stares in his direction started a cold sweat dripping down Rockshoalman's back. Spirits, he hated crowds. His dark wavy hair and deep umber-brown eyes a stark contrast to the light-eyed, pale Danish highborn. Frozen in time at twenty-two, his bachelor status and fame made him a prime target for the marriage brokers of the area. Only his reputation as an aloof and eccentric artist saved him from the Matrons seeking a match for their daughters.

"We cannot stay," Rockshoalman whispered. "My presence puts all these people in danger."

"Nonsense."

"The demon will sense me." Hands twisted together. The high wing-tipped collar tightened with each nervous breath.

"Your demon cannot find you here, Domnule." The deep baritone of Ciprian carried only to him. A great bear of a man, with the thick black hair and short-cropped beard typical of the Romani, he should draw attention. His Guardian never did. A constant shadow no one paid attention to, but one always ready to protect Rockshoalman and his power charged paintings.

"The paintings—"

"Are safe," Ciprian chided him.

His works were the only reason Rockshoalman attended Mestre Poulsen's party. To make sure death remained only the subject of his art, not a personification brought to life.

Music drifted down the polished wood and marble stairs to fill the limited space not populated with silk bedecked ladies and black tuxedoed lords. But nothing could drown out the hum of power from his paintings. A hum sure to call the demon.

"I never should have agreed to the banker's request to show my latest masterworks."

The dusky golden pools of Ciprian's eyes, ageless in their own way, stared at him calmly and gestured toward the central staircase. Rockshoalman sighed. They had this argument many times before. Each time, he lost.

"I know. The funds from tonight's display provided an escape into another identity." Rockshoalman had outlived this one.

"True, we must soon leave this persona behind, but not quite yet." A knowing curve teased at a corner of Ciprian's mouth. "There is one more task to accomplish."

What task, Ciprian refused to say. No matter how much Rockshoalman badgered him since the invitation arrived two weeks past. Had Ciprian received a vision with his *Second Sight*? The joyous laughter of young children off to his left startled Rockshoalman upon reaching the second story landing. Servants shushed them while herding them down the main hallway and away from the party, but could not dampen their innocent exuberance. A pang of regret painted yet another layer of darkness over his heart.

Rockshoalman paused before the intricately carved double doors of the ballroom. Open and inviting, the music flowing through them beckoned guests inside. Murmured conversations mixed with the energy emanating from his paintings to swirl within the gold-leafed dome ceiling. He pulled Ciprian to the side. Any excuse to delay his appearance.

"Power fills this manse. My works may have already drawn *Him* forth." Undetectable except by another cursed immortal like himself or one gifted with the *Second Sight* like Ciprian, his demon could mimic any person's form.

"The night's dalliance will see us gone by morning. Not time enough for him to find you," Ciprian whispered, his voice calm and firm.

Energy pulsed within the ballroom. Fiery. Passionate. One not connected to his paintings. Rockshoalman's gaze danced from one person to another. Searching. Fearing what he might find. Yet only mortals appeared before him. Had the demon found a way to deceive them? He frowned. No. This was different.

Death was a compelling subject to paint—and his immortal curse. But Rockshoalman had found a loophole. These works, unlike the abominations of his curse, captured the serenity found in that darkest of moments, the cathartic release of pain through grief and the hope of a new life beyond. The emotions locked within the very brushstrokes of each piece. On rare occasions he had even met individuals who saw the beauty within the paintings as he did. Is that what he sensed? Someone responding to his works with a gift of their own?

"Wards protect the paintings from detection, just as my presence protects you."

Rockshoalman studied the patrons standing near the art displayed around the ballroom. The balcony dripped with people attempting to avoid the crowded dance floor yet get a glimpse of his famed paintings. "Perhaps."

A tendril of vitality teased at his senses like the warmth of the sun upon his cheek during a winter's day. He turned his head towards the pull. Her hair shimmered in the candlelight, spun gold with bright pink flowers plaited in the braids. The azure blue gown a slice of sky floating above the polished white marble floors as though the clouds themselves carried her. Rapture infused her whole being as she gazed upon the *Isle of the Dead*.

He could not look away. Captured as surely as the emotions he imbued into his paintings. She could not be older than sixteen or seventeen—a mere blink of time compared to his centuries. Yet…his heart lightened at the sight of her.

A gentle touch from Ciprian broke the trance. Stepping to the front, Ciprian made final adjustments to Rockshoalman's attire. "Release your fears, my friend. Learn to live again."

Rockshoalman let out a ragged breath. "I no longer know how." Centuries of unending time with no hope for release had taken its toll. He only remembered the pain now.

Ciprian gripped Rockshoalman's arm. The matching white ink tattoos hidden under their clothing surged. Rockshoalman inhaled.

Clean, crisp mountain air, the kind found right after a fresh snowfall, filled his lungs. With it, a sense of unblemished innocence. Pure joy of life flowed from his Guardian like a river. Infectious,

Rockshoalman found his shoulders relaxing in his fitted frock coat, the tightness of his chest beneath the black silk waistcoat easing, and even a smile tugged at the corner of his mouth. Such was the ability of Guardian to Immortal Charge through the white ink. Safety. Healing. Peace.

"Worry not. You will learn once more," Ciprian stated with a wink, releasing their connection. Pressing a small item into Rockshoalman's palm, his Guardian disappeared into the crowded sea of black formal attire expected of all men in this age. One might expect the Romani to lumber. Instead, three decades of dancing with women—and daggers—allowed him to glide through crowds with grace and deftness, disappearing from memory. A skill Rockshoalman wished he possessed. The disappearing part, at least.

So many people. Chest tightening, the laugher of people around him taunted him; happiness he longed to have. Shoulders pressed hard against the wooden threshold, one foot in the light, one in the darkness, the etched wood design dragged at his coat, as though preventing him from entering the hall.

"Spirits help me," he whispered.

His palm warmed, and he looked down at the smooth pink quartz glowing faintly in the candlelight. His worry stone. A smile came with ease this time.

Out of sight, but never unprotected.

"Thank you, my friend."

Clenching the stone tighter, Ciprian's calming energy imbued into the crystal washed through him, loosening tense muscles and banishing the anxiety back to its dark, cursed hole. Taking a deep breath, the rosy, citrus scent of the peony garland in the flower-adorned archway soothed frayed nerves. Rockshoalman stepped through. He searched the crowd gathered below his premier painting, but the girl must have moved on to another painting. It should not matter. It did. He shook his head, dismissing the need to find her. He did not *need* anyone. Immortality had erased that. Nodding to those who greeted him, Rockshoalman moved as though he had a destination, even when he had none.

Long had it been since he mingled amongst the highborn of Denmark. Hiding in plain sight for so long, the skill to blend into any culture was second nature now. Here was no different from the myriad other countries he had lived in over the centuries. Customs may change over generations, but some things, like curiosity of the unusual, stayed the same. Rockshoalman frowned. His body trapped in stasis at just over two decades in age, survival depended on changing his appearance, giving the illusion of aging even when he never did, the manipulating of people's perception a necessary lie. One he despised.

He preferred the quiet of his studio, but the people needed to see him alive before he could convince them of his mortality. His 'death' would increase the value of the entire art collection inherited by his next incarnation—an apprentice of the Master—thus immortalizing the cycle of existence without truly living.

"Corrado," Mestre Poulsen hailed, moving with swift strides towards him. Rockshoalman smoothed his black frock coat and straightened his white bow tie.

Dressed in similar attire, his host's cashmere trousers were of a finer quality than Rockshoalman's, but the button-up boots were dull and dingy. He glanced at his own boots, polished to a high shine.

The portly lord of the manse stretched out his sweaty hand before remembering that Rockshoalman, or Master Corrado Lee as they knew him here, did not touch people. An idiosyncrasy people accepted from the famous painter.

"I am pleased you accepted my invitation." He pointed to the paintings displayed on the high walls, each piece cordoned off by golden ropes. "Protected as you requested, yet visible for all to partake of their…most unusual subject."

Oddity. Rockshoalman heard the unspoken word. Yet that same oddity drew demand and with it, coin.

"The placement is sufficient," Rockshoalman conceded. No one must touch his paintings. The emotional backlash a natural person suffered from contact could kill them. Never again would Rockshoalman suffer that agony. The lord of the manor hesitated, his brows drawing together.

Rockshoalman sighed inside. He hated stroking egos, but those same egos paid him coin so he and his protectors might live—and disappear as necessary. "Thank you for allowing me to present my art to so many. I am glad my trifling works have enlivened your party."

"Trifling, he calls some of the greatest pieces I have had the pleasure to view." Mestre Poulsen scoffed to all those near. "You honor me by allowing me to showcase your collection during such a special occasion."

Rockshoalman bowed. "The honor is all mine."

Now preening like a peacock, his host smiled and waved Rockshoalman further into the ballroom. "Come. Let me introduce you to the other investors."

Following the Dane, Rockshoalman linked his wrists behind him, lest someone else forget his aversion, and attempt to shake hands, the worry stone in his left hand, a cool, smooth pool of serenity in an ocean of chaos. Making all the correct bows and small talk, he allowed Mestre Poulsen his moment to glow within the presence of his peers.

"I am so pleased you attended tonight," Mestre Poulson rambled. "We spared no expense with the decorations, wanting to do justice to your paintings."

"Your patronage is much appreciated, Mestre."

The Great Hall blazed with the warmth of a thousand dancing lights. Silver sconces hung on marble columns, the drip of beeswax candles captured by silver discs at their base, protecting patrons and strings of reflective beads alike. The crystals of the high chandelier scattered dancing fairies of light across the multitudes beneath them as though the children of light tiptoed among a field of vibrant flowers.

"Maybe we can even entice you to a dance or two with the flowers of the ball tonight?" Mestre Poulson gestured to the multitude of ladies who noted their passing with skittish glances.

"We shall see."

The ladies in their silks and satins did seem a garden of flowers, each one more beautiful and vibrant than the last. And like flowers, simple cold chased them away.

Cold. One of the many names society called Rockshoalman. Aloof. Eccentric. *Foreign.* A spot of darkness amongst the light. He brushed a hand across his short hair, ducking his head to hide from the stares before he caught himself and stiffened. Pale eyes, bright with the joys of life, sparkled in the candlelight all around him. His almost black ones reflected eons of darkness. Caught up in their lives, lives that would end one day, they did not understand the eternal isolation he suffered.

Most watched him with a mixture of awe, curiosity, and sometimes even fear. Rockshoalman ignored them, using each evasion to cast another layer of armor around his heart, telling himself their disinterest didn't matter. Being alone, his solitary life a defense against the pain of loneliness, he only needed to concern himself with his unending existence. He had stopped living centuries ago.

The last group, a collection of Mestre Poulsen's banking colleagues, engaged Rockshoalman in discussions of potential commissions until a petite ball of energy bounded into their midst. The same pulse of life he had felt before. Energy he hadn't realized he missed.

"Papa." The youthful girl hugged her father before turning to stare at Rockshoalman. "Oh…" Crystal blue eyes perched in a round face of porcelain skin stared into his. Her lips parted slightly and spread into a smile so bright it stole Rockshoalman's breath. "Forgive my poor manners." She curtseyed and bowed her head. Although coifed and bejeweled, the gold of her hair seemed to glow, as if touched by fire from within. Rockshoalman's mind started mixing paint colors in his head, knowing he would never come close to capturing the pure hue before him.

"I did not know you were with a stranger, father."

Mestre Poulsen chuckled. "Ah, dear Elsabeth. Even had you known it would not have stopped your enthusiasm." Tucking his blushing daughter's hand within the crook of his elbow, the lord turned to Rockshoalman. "Elsabeth, please greet Herre Corrado Lee, master painter and my guest of honor tonight. Herre Corrado, may I present my youngest and most energetic daughter, Elsabeth. Tis her coming of age and presentation to society, we celebrate tonight."

"So, it is your works that grace my celebration. A double pleasure to meet you, Herre Corrado." She extended her hand.

Before her father could say anything, Rockshoalman grasped the dainty fingers. Raising her knuckles to his lips, he brushed the lightest of kisses across silky smooth skin. Energy flowed through him, reminiscent of Ciprian's gift. Life. Innocence. And something more he could not name.

She shivered within his grasp as though a connection passed between them in that brief moment. Maybe it had. The warmth of her hand within his and the light rosy scent of the pink peonies in her hair teased awake his senses.

"The pleasure is mine, Froken Elsabeth." Her smile enticed one from him. "Please, call me Corrado. I am no lord. Only a simple painter who enjoys the beauty life sometimes grants me to put on canvas."

Human touch. He had forgotten the pleasure it brought. The sensation of escaping from a cold wintery night into a fire-warmed room invigorated him. His skin burned from her heat. Her beauty etched an image he longed to paint.

Except he only painted death.

His smile faded. Rockshoalman released her hand, the chill of loss created within him an ache he thought long gone. They were worlds apart. She would not want to spend her time with him, as he had nothing to offer. Yet, the yearning remained. His gaze sought hers if only to imprint her image in his mind for all eternity. A puzzled look stole across her face but brightened after only a momentary pause.

"If he is our guest, Father, then surely it is the duty of our family to entertain Herre…" She glanced his way, smiling. "…to entertain Corrado."

"Well, yes." Mestre Poulsen hesitated, flustered by his daughter's brashness and by Rockshoalman's own actions.

"Mestre Poulsen, would you allow me the honor of a dance with your beautiful daughter?" Slipping the worry stone into his waistcoat pocket, he held out his hand, wanting, no *needing* to feel the fire she evoked in him once more.

"Without a doubt, he would. Is that not so, Father?" Pushing up on her tiptoes, she kissed her father's cheek before he could respond any other way. "I would not want to seem rude to our guest."

Rockshoalman smothered his smile. Elsabeth's subtle manipulation of the situation, to get exactly what she wanted, fascinated him in one so young. Ciprian could take lessons from this young slip of a girl.

"Oh, no. We mustn't have that. Please, Corrado, would you be so kind as to accord my daughter a dance?" He offered his daughter's hand. "I'm sure we can rearrange her dance card."

Rockshoalman bowed before accepting. "If you insist."

The glimmer of mischief in Elsabeth's eyes spoke volumes. With this one, he must watch his step lest he find himself the focus of her next set of plans. Ciprian appeared out of the shadows, his smile bright as he took in Rockshoalman's companion. Ciprian nodded. Rockshoalman stumbled to a stop.

"Is something wrong, Corrado?" Elsabeth tightened her grasp, an act of comfort.

'You will learn to live again.'

The *Second Sight*. Ciprian must have foreseen this meeting—the last task his Guardian refused to tell him about lest he disrupt Fate's plan from occurring.

"No, my dear." Rockshoalman collected her hands within his. The connection flowed outward, making every sense expand to inspired heights. The burning warmth of her touch beneath his, the light lilac scent of her perfume, the soft sounds of her breath cresting over the pale pink wetness of her lips—each sight, sound, and touch experienced again as if for the first time.

"Everything is fine, as long as I am with you." But would she want to stay with him?

His words provoked another blush, but Elsabeth never dropped her gaze. The bright blue of her eyes, innocent depths more profound than any ocean, consumed him. "I think I would like that possibility...to stay with you." She pulled one of the pink flowers from her hair and offered it to him. "If you would have me."

Such strength. Elsabeth would need all of that moxie if she chose to stand by his side for longer than one night, for she would have to leave this current life and her family behind when he next disappeared.

The sweet scent of the peony bloomed between them—a challenge. Rockshoalman need only accept it. Years of pain and loneliness twisted in a vice-like grip around his chest. Could he condemn her to a life of death? No. He pulled back. She tightened her grip, holding him still.

"Do not be afraid."

"You do not know what you are asking. My...life is not one without difficulty."

"I know." She glanced over at his paintings. "But you have discovered the beauty it offers despite that…difficulty." Elsabeth's smile beamed up at him. She might be young in age, but the eyes that stared back at him contained an old soul, one who somehow understood.

Rockshoalman inhaled the scent of the proffered flower—its scent forevermore linked to Elsabeth—before tucking the pink bud into his lapel. Elsabeth's smile brightened. As did his heart.

He cleared his throat. "I believe you wished to dance."

"Yes, please." The fervent sound of her voice set his heart to racing.

He nodded to Ciprian. Leading Elsabeth to the dance floor, he wrapped his hand around her waist just as a soft piano waltz began. Notes swirled around them, quiet at first, then gaining volume as the strings picked up the melody. The music whispered its song to Rockshoalman, the minor chords mixing with the major to produce a beauty he felt the girl in his arms embodied.

Life.

A thirst Rockshoalman forgot he once possessed grew. Energy surged back and forth between them in time to the dance, a dance he never intended to start, but now could not imagine ever stopping. Cracks in the barrier around his heart appeared. Elsabeth grinned up at him, shattering the defenses he set centuries ago. How he did not know, but with nothing more than a smile, her pure innocence crumbled his jaded resistance. How had such a simple act, a dance, opened up so many possibilities?

"What have you done to me," he whispered.

"Danced to the song."

"What song?"

"The song of my heart."

Mirroring the one now dancing in his.

Spinning across the white marble, the silk of her gown swished like a soft whisper in his ear. *Live,* it said. Captured in her gaze, her warmth chasing the last chill of fear from him, Rockshoalman found something else he long thought lost.

Hope. And a future.

Part III

The Future

Rockshoalman opened his eyes. Once again in the present, he stood in the center of the ballroom ruins. The music still echoed around him. Stars replaced the candles and a full moon cast its glow into the roofless room. No people remained from that time. Even the building held on by a thin thread. Fire destroyed the back half of the manse over a half-century ago, yet left the foundation and most of the marble walls and floor of the ballroom intact. Moving about the room, he swayed to the memory of the music. Footprints marked his passage in the soot-ladened muck glazing the stone floor.

Still, he danced.

His hands warmed as if that same full of life girl graced his arms once more. She had opened up his heart to an unexplored world that night. Less than six months later, she taught him what it meant to be alive once more by agreeing to share the rest of her life with him.

Immortality was not the focus on death; it was the ability to embrace life. To see the beauty surrounding him, to dance to the music of the world, to touch the experiences life offered. It took a girl who lived only a fraction of the time he existed to show him how.

His feet shuffled to a stop. The music faded away, but the night whispered to him still.

Live.

The manse creaked with soft footfalls. Rockshoalman smiled. She had come.

"Robert?" Kyrissa Spears stood in the doorway, arms wrapped tight around her chest, the cast iron lantern flickering its feeble light at her feet. "I know you said you wanted to be alone and to wait in the carriage, but…I…well, something told me to come find you." She shook her head. "It was so soft, like a whisper in the wind, but I thought you called me."

Love.

Someone *had* called her, but not him. No wonder Lucien had insisted she accompany him tonight. Had his Guardian known?

"I'm sorry, I'll go—"

"Stay." Raising the same hand he once offered to another dance partner a century ago, he reveled in the magic of fate that had brought Kyrissa to him. Elsabeth had taught him love appeared when you most needed it—just as Kyrissa had shown up in his life when he had lost all hope. First, as a student, learning to cope with a painting gift like his. Then as a lover to save him from his curse.

"Come dance with me."

A frown creased her forehead. "Here?"

"Yes."

A smile crept out, one reminiscent of another fair-haired woman. Breath clogged his throat. Just as he had the first time they made love, his mind raced to paint Kyrissa, to capture the look of pure love she offered to him. A chuckle bubbled up from his chest. He had been brooding about Elsabeth the first time he had met Kyrissa. Once again, Kyrissa's presence filled the void left by another.

"There isn't any music," Kyrissa teased. She had taken her hair out of its customary ponytail, the long golden strands free flowing around her shoulders. He liked it that way.

"We will have to make our own then." Grasping her hand, he spun her in a pirouette, her laughter echoing against the marble walls. Folding her into his arms, Rockshoalman, or Robert Shoalman as she knew him in this lifetime, waltzed back and forth across the floor.

They danced in silence for a few minutes until Kyrissa stopped him, staring off toward a dark corner. "What is it?" The hair on the nape of his neck prickled.

"The locals say this place is haunted."

He shook his head. "The locals like to have their fun with tourists. A haunted manse lends to the mysterious air of the area."

"But the fire here. What caused it?"

"Treasure hunters." He kissed away her confused look. "This was once a storage place for some of my paintings after I inherited the property. The fire was…unavoidable." A stab of remembered pain, the days of forced painting because of their destruction, stole his voice. The Romani thought they were protecting him by keeping the paintings from his demon. Their act cost them their lives. Ciprian's life.

Soft hands caressed his face. Kyrissa's touch, her power, a balm pulling him back from the brink of darkness. He kissed her palms and danced once more.

"This place must have been beautiful during its peak."

"It was, although at the time I did not notice. More to my regret." After the fire, he could not bear to return, allowing the manse to fall into indifferent neglect. Much like his heart. "Now I must decide what to do with the place." She searched his face. Intelligence blazed behind her jade green eyes, asking questions he was not ready to answer. Twirling her about, Rockshoalman attempted to distract Kyrissa. She caught his wrist, stroking the burn scars. He swallowed.

He was not fooling her at all.

"How long ago were you here?"

"Almost a century and several lifetimes ago."

"Could you restore it?"

Rockshoalman stilled. He could. But did he want to? This belonged to the past. Then again, so did he. "I…"

"This is where you met her, isn't it? Elsabeth?"

"How did you…"

Wide eyes stared over his shoulder. Kyrissa rubbed at the goosebumps breaking out across her arms. "I think…I think I just saw her."

Rockshoalman's breath caught. Spinning, he searched the darkness. Lamplight threw dancing shadows on the gold-fleck marble. Cobwebs thicker than cotton candy fluttered in the evening breeze. Silence. Disappointment left him feeling foolish. Her spirit still lingered within this place, but had he actually expected to see a ghost?

"You have been listening to the villagers too much." A chill whipped in through the broken roof and he shivered. "Maybe we should go."

"Why did you come here, Robert?"

"I told you. I need to decide what to do with the place."

"Really? That's what you're going to go with?" A hand hitched on her hip, Kyrissa cocked one eyebrow. "You know you're a terrible liar." She gathered his hands in hers. Warmth surrounded him. "What's the actual reason?"

How could he explain? How could he tell Kyrissa he needed to say goodbye to a ghost before he could ever wholly open his heart again? She knew about Elsabeth. Well, most of the story. She had needed to understand his reluctance, his guilt about loving her, even though Elsabeth had died several lifetimes ago. He turned to look out the windowless gaps in the wall. Shoving his hands into his pockets, he grasped the worry stone, the carved symbol on one side rough against his thumb.

"It is an insane idea."

Strong arms wrapped around him from behind, her chin perched on his shoulder. He leaned into her touch.

"After everything I have seen, demons and dark immortals, mystical auras and angelic singing, ink that can heal or kill—not to mention my own ability to kill people with my paintings—you think anything you tell me is more insane than all that?"

He snorted. "When you put it that way." Turning and enfolding her within his arms, he couldn't help comparing Kyrissa's physical and mental strength to Elsabeth's gentle support and guidance. They both possessed an aura of power that anchored him in the storm that was his cursed immortal life—each saving his soul a century apart from one another. Where

Elsabeth could quell his broody moods with a glance, Kyrissa called him out verbally. Could he release that part of his heart that lived in the past to Kyrissa?

Rockshoalman heaved a strained breath out. "I came to say goodbye. However, I am unsure of how to do so. This place..." A lump lodged in his throat. Loss and guilt twisted at his heart, yet happiness and love fought back. "Do I leave the past behind for good, destroy this place, or remember the happiness by restoring the manse so that others might also experience that joy?"

"You came to ask her," Kyrissa stated, a soft smile on her face.

Rockshoalman shrugged. "I told you it was insane." Pulling her tighter against his chest, he started swaying.

"What's that tune?"

He stared at her. "What tune?"

Kyrissa hummed the song. Music from his memory. His pulse raced even as he held his breath. The music was only in his head. Wasn't it?

"Sound carries up from the valley. I could hear the villagers singing earlier." Even as he tried to explain the improbability away, he too heard the strains of music. "It is not possible."

Kyrissa cocked her head to the side, walking over to a window. "Robert." She turned to look at him. "The sound isn't coming from outside. It's here, in this room."

The sweet perfume of peonies grew more intense as the moon crested over the edge of the missing roof. A beam of moonlight pulsed through the ancient chandelier crystals, sending dancing fairy lights over a corner of the darkness. Gold glinted above a pale blue shimmer. Kyrissa inhaled sharply behind him.

A figure stood silent, frozen in time.

"Elsabeth." His whisper fogged the frosty air in front of him.

"You see her too?" Kyrissa moved closer and grasped his arm, but her voice held no fear.

"Yes."

"Okay. Good. Means I'm not insane." Kyrissa took a slow, deep breath. "Guess I get to add seeing ghosts to that list I mentioned earlier."

The visage curtsied, then danced across the ballroom floor. A white mist followed the ethereal figure, creating a proper dance in the clouds. Rockshoalman's heart hammered against his ribs as she neared. She held out a dainty hand in greeting.

He came to talk to her, positive her spirit remained because of the flower in the barren garden, yet never expected Elsabeth would manifest to him like this. Rockshoalman stood frozen. "What do I do?"

"What did you do when you first met her?" Kyrissa asked.

"I kissed her hand."

"Well." Kyrissa gestured to the outstretched hand hovering before them.

"But she is…" Did Elsabeth know she was a ghost? "How would that work?"

"I assume the same way a kiss always works," Kyrissa's tone mocked. He threw her one of his famed glares, which as

76

usual, just had her fighting more amusement. "It can't hurt to try, can it?"

She had a point.

Rockshoalman bent at the waist, lifting his hand to raise the delicate, ghostly fingers to his lips. A tingle of energy, not unlike that of his first meeting with Elsabeth, caressed his mouth. The shock of the sensation had him stepping back. Guilt washed over him. Had she never met him, Elsabeth might have lived longer. "I should have protected you. If not for me—"

Tendrils of energy stopped his apology as she placed two fingers over his lips.

"I am sorry," he whispered.

The image smiled and shook her head. Both hands covered her heart, her smile bright and joyous.

"She loved you, Robert. That's all that mattered to her."

The ghost pointed to him and then to Kyrissa before bringing her hands together. Pressing her finger to her lips, she blew kisses to them both. Joyous laughter, a sound he had not heard in ages echoed as the figure danced away, dissolving into a thousand sparkling flecks of moonlight.

"Wait." Rockshoalman rushed over, but she had disappeared. He spun in the moonbeam, searching, but even that faded as the moon rose higher. "What do I need to do? You did not tell me."

"I think she did." Kyrissa bent down to retrieve an item from the floor. A small pink peony. One that matched the flower in his lapel.

Elsabeth's favorite.

He stared at the bloom and remembered the bouquets that filled the manse and lined every archway. Laughter and music had lifted the spirits of all the guests, both young and old, and happiness filled the manse that night. A happiness he yearned to enjoy once again.

"Maybe this was her way of saying goodbye."

"No." He took the flower and tucked it in Kyrissa hair. "This was her reminding me how to live." He kissed Kyrissa deeply, pulling her into a tight embrace. Breaking the kiss, she wrapped her arm about his waist, laying her head on his shoulder. One last glimmer of blue-tinged moonlight hovered before him.

Adio, Elsabeth.

Much as Elsabeth had done the first night they met, the fading spirit broke down the remaining walls around his heart. Letting his final bit of guilt dissolve into the moonlight, Rockshoalman bid farewell to his first love and welcomed Kyrissa into his heart for the rest of eternity.

"I see why you loved her." Kyrissa wiped away a single tear from his cheek. Her own eyes misty in the dim light. "I'm glad I got to meet her, although no one is going to ever believe me and Mandy will be so pissed she wasn't here to get a picture."

"I was here and I am not sure I believe it."

Kyrissa looked around. "Is she gone?"

Rockshoalman closed his eyes for a moment. Gone was the darkness and despair he first felt upon entering the grounds. Only serenity remained; the ghosts of the past finally at peace. Opening his eyes, love washed over him. "She is at rest." He placed a hand over his heart. "But she will live on."

"You're going to restore the manse?"

"Yes. For her and for you."

"Good. You know, once you restore this place, it would be a superb place to hold a wedding."

"Is that so?" Rockshoalman could almost hear the gears of design spinning in Kyrissa's head as she looked around. She respected his need to reclaim the past, but always added her own artistic flair to any restoration project they developed. He grinned. This place would be theirs together; past and present reshaped for the future.

Kyrissa grinned at him, her eyes a deep amorous jade. "How long do you think the restoration will take?"

"Depends on who wants to get married here. If you are talking about Mandy, eons."

Kyrissa laughed. "And if I had someone else in mind?"

Rockshoalman smiled, nuzzling her hair and drinking in her perfume along with the delicately sweet scent of the flower over her ear. Might he finally have his answer? He chuckled, realizing he already did.

"As soon as that someone wants."

He would restore the house to its former glory in Elsabeth's memory. Her presence no longer graced his side, but she would be forever in his heart. Past and present no longer had to be separate; the two forever entwined within this place.

He missed Elsabeth, but thanks to her dance, he would never dance alone again.

WHO IS KIRA DECKER

Being the youngest of five kids, my oldest sister introduced me to the wonderful adventure books offered at a very young age, and I haven't finished the trip yet. Only now, it's my own characters leading me through sword fights, growing pains, supernatural beings, and of course, love of a happily ever after ending.

I am an avid reader of Science Fiction, Fantasy, Adult, NA and YA. The characters I had knocking around in my head since I was young decided they wanted someone to tell their story. Thankfully, they chose me.

The journey has been an exciting one. I managed to find a critique/writing partner who thinks like me (the world will never be the same) and who pushes me to new levels in my writing. I love to let my characters lead me where they will, but she managed to sneak in a little bit of plotting into my writing toolbox.

I have wonderful supportive husband and three great kids who give me as much time as they can to devote to writing. The cat however demands my lap time and won't take no for an answer.

When not writing, I have acted as a volunteer parent coach for my daughter's cheerleading - only holding my breath once in a while when she does new flying stunts - watch my youngest son delve into computer programing and build amazing Lego inventions, and help my oldest son navigate his own adventures in adulting (Yes, I use him as research for my NA stories). I even decided to gain certification as an Emergency Medical Technician (EMT), a goal I have had since high school.

My loving husband encourages me in everything I do. He is my go-to-guy for historical facts about weapons and warfare tactics, as well as, my devil's advocate in my world building (No I do not have sparkly zombie werewolves in my world, dear). He is such a source of love and inspiration that romance always find its way into my stories.

After all, he is my Happy Ever After.

I adore the ride my characters take me on and
I hope you enjoy my stories as much as I love writing them.

WHERE TO FIND ME

Want to follow my adventures and get updates on my writing projects? Follow me on your nearest social media.

Twitter: @kiradecker

FaceBook: Kira Decker

                KiraDeckerBooks

Instagram: KiraDecker

Goodreads: KiraDecker

I love to hear from my readers.

Email: authorkiradecker@gmail.com

Liked what your read?

Reviews are precious gifts to an author. Let me know what you think by leaving a review on your favorite book site.

Also By Kira Decker

Amazon Page: Kira Decker Page

TRANSCENDENCE

Academy of the Dead Anthology © 2020

Young Adult, Supernatural, Paranormal

High School -
Where exams are killers and so are the students

Starting over at a new high school is never easy, especially senior year, but for Dean Eldritch it's way better than the alternative—jail. With his twin sister, Samarah, and the help of Jynixis "Jynx" Jaehne, a feisty player in this new school, maybe this time he can get through the year without killing anyone.

Ghosts haunt Dean—ones only he can hear and see—as he struggles to overcome his past failings and guilt. A process made more difficult when Jynx turns from a potential ally into a complicated witness to his death filed crimes.

When Dean realizes Samarah could be trapped forever, Jynx offers him a choice. Help Jynx pass her final exams or she sends him to jail for murder and Samarah never escapes.

For at Transcendence, if you fail, you die.

Also available writing as Toni Decker

Amazon Page: Toni Decker Page

The Shoalman Chronicles Series - New Adult, Paranormal Romance/Urban Fantasy The original world of the Guardians and the Immortal they protect

Images Eternal © – Book 1
If Images are worth a thousand words, hers sing a thousand Eternal songs

Shoalman Immortal © – Book 2
Falling in love was never supposed to part of the picture

Dark Ink Embrace © – Book 3
His gift connects them. Her touch unlocks their fate.

White Ink Surrender © – Book 4 (Coming Soon)

Sneak Peek

of

TRANSCENDENCE

by

Kira Decker

Part of the

Academy of the Dead

Anthology

Chapter 1

Ever see a ghost?

Most people would answer no. Most people weren't Dean Eldritch.

The ability to see, and in his case, hear ghosts would probably be interesting if it weren't for his twin sister, Samarah. Her constant interference and incessant bubbliness with the whole idea took annoying to another level. One he currently wasn't in the mood to deal with.

"What do you think the new school will be like?" Sam twirled around him, delighted with the adventure.

"I don't know." Dean adjusted his backpack to the other shoulder, shuffling along behind the other kids walking towards an institutional white, two-story building with slate grey metal windows.

"Not much to look at." Sam sneered and crossed her arms. "I thought Mom and Dad said this was some special elite school."

"I said, I don't know. It's school. The same sucky classes and teenage drama as any other school." Dean raked a hand through his short, brownish hair. A new school meant he was starting over. Again. At least it wasn't jail.

His deep sigh plumed in the crisp winter air, creating a fog as ethereal as his ghosts. He snugged the leather jacket tighter around his neck against the chill. What had his parents said? A fresh start. A clean slate without all the emotional baggage for his senior year of high school. Yeah right. Baggage traveled with you. His was just more transparent.

"What classes do you think we'll have?"

"We?" Dean stopped short. Two students hurried by but paid him no mind.

"Are you seriously going to be in all my classes?"

"Why not? I can be the fun one, and you can be your normal broody self. You know, the mysterious new guy with some dark cloud hanging over him." Sam imitated a doom cloud over his head. Dean flapped his hands to make her stop.

"Promise me you'll be quiet. I have enough crap going on without you running your mouth and getting me in trouble."

"Promise." Sam mimed zipping and locking her mouth before throwing away the key. Dean rolled his eyes. She would never last. She never did.

A bell rang in the distance. Dean joined the rush of students entering the front entrance. A mild electrical charge zapped him as he passed the threshold, while Sam let out a string of muttered curses behind him.

"Oh, don't mind dubbie. You get used to it after a while." A girl pushed open the next set of doors ahead of them and held it open for him to pass.

"Thanks. Um, who or what is a dubbie?"

The girl side-eyed him like he'd asked the stupidest question on the planet. "The dybbuk barrier. You know, to protect us. We all just call it dubbie because it has a

5

life of its own." She laughed. Dean smiled but missed the joke.

"You must be new."

"Yeah." Dean shuffled his feet. "Moved here last week."

"And you got in here as a senior?" Her gaze inspected him from head to toe as if he had mutated in the past few minutes. "Wow. You must be good."

"I can hold my own." Dean raised his chin and squared his shoulders. His sister's presence hanging behind him swelled his confidence even more.

"I bet you can. Come on, I'll show you where the office is." One more quizzical look, a half-smile, and the girl spun on her heel to stroll through the large open atrium.

"After that look, I'd say she wants you to hold more than your own," Sam whispered in his ear.

"Shut up."

Sam chuckled. "This will be fun."

Horror show was more like it. Just like the rest of his life.

*****

Coming to Kindle Unlimited